C902180963

LIBRARIES NI
WITHDRAWN FROM STOCK

LIBRARIES NI
WITHDRAWN FROM STOCK

D1492989

Other Titles Available:

 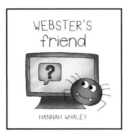 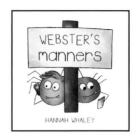

For Layla and Iris

Published by Born Digital Books.

www.borndigitalbooks.co.uk

Text © 2015 by Hannah Whaley.
Illustrations © 2015 by Hannah Whaley.
All rights reserved.

No part of this publication may be reproduced, distributed, or transmitted in any form or by any means, including photocopying, recording, or other electronic or mechanical methods, without the prior written permission of the publisher. The moral rights of the author have been asserted.

First printing: January 2015.
Rudiment Font © Kevin Richey

ISBN-13: 978-0-9930012-3-9

Webster's Bedtime

Written and Illustrated
by Hannah Whaley

Webster loved playing with technology toys.
He stayed up late making lots of noise.

When Mummy called "Bedtime!"
he didn't want to sleep.
"If you let me stay up, I won't make a peep!"

The whole room sighed;
all at once his toys said...

"We're ever so tired...
won't you please go to bed?"

Oh what a shock!

Webster jumped with a fright!

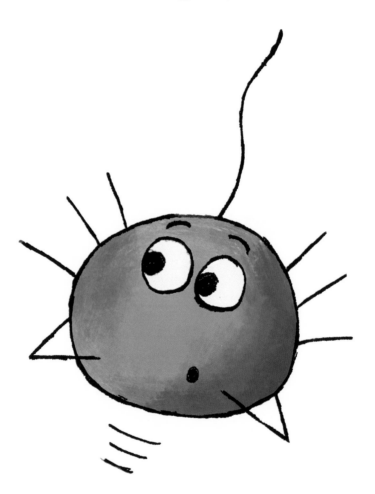

"You mean YOU go to sleep TOO when its night?"

"Oh yes", said the TV with a great big yawn.
"We have to recharge our batteries by dawn.

All day we sing and we flash and we beep
but it's nighttime now, so can we please get
some sleep?"

Webster blinked and rubbed his eyes.
This news had come as quite a surprise.

"I have an idea!" he
suddenly yelped.

"If you can't get to sleep then
perhaps I can help!"

"I can read
you a story,

I can sing
you a song,

I can tuck you in so you're
snug all night long!"

"That's not how we work", said the
phone with a frown.

"You'll need to figure out
how to power us all down."

Webster wanted to help them now.
"I can do it," he said, "I think I know how."

Goodnight games consoles, we had
great fun today. As he pressed each
button, the lights faded away.

Goodnight, sleep tight, my new DVD.
With a zap of the remote
he turned off the TV.

Goodnight mobile phone,
no more texting tonight.

He tapped the screen
and off went its light.

Goodnight laptop, all your emails are sent.
He pulled down the lid, off to sleep it went.

Goodnight computer, it's time to dream.
He leaned over the desk
and switched off the screen.

Goodnight tablet and my favourite app.

With one swish of his finger it was taking a nap.

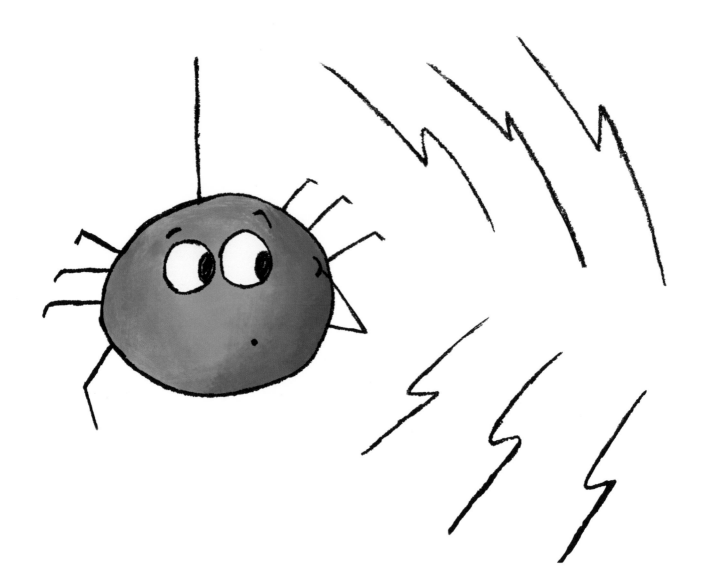

Webster switched off all the technology toys, yet still he could hear a thundering noise...

The TV was making an almighty snore!

He turned down the volume
and slipped out the door.

Out into the hallway where he
heard something squawking...

It was the mobile phone –
it had started sleep talking!
He hushed the phone with a gentle stroke...

...but as he did that, the tablet awoke.
With a whimper, a cry and a tiny scream,
the poor little tablet had a bad dream!

Back into its cover, all snuggled and cozy
It wasn't the only one now feeling dozy!

But laptop complained "Computer keeps me awake!". Zzzzzz typed Webster until not a sound did it make.

And when games consoles sleepwalked every
which way, Webster ushered them back
and asked them to stay.

Finally peaceful, there was silence at last.
Webster could feel his eyes closing fast.

It was late and he felt like a sleepy head.

He yawned and he stretched
and he climbed into bed.

No more ringing or tweeting
or flashing or beeps.
Before Webster knew it he was fast asleep.

Mummy tucked him in and said
"Good Nighty Night Night."

Then she flicked one last switch and turned out the light.

19694721R00022

Printed in Poland
by Amazon Fulfillment
Poland Sp. z o.o., Wrocław